THE RUNAWAY POKÉMON

Adapted by Simcha Whitehill
from the episode "Piplup, Up and Away!"

ISBN 978-0-545-34172-1

©2011 Pokémon. ©1997-2011 Nintendo, Creatures, GAME FREAK...
Pokémon properties are trademarks of Ni...
Published by Scholastic Inc.
SCHOLASTIC and associated logos are trademarks and/or register...

12 11 10 9 8 7 6 5 4 3 2 1   11 12 13 14 15/0

Designed by Cheung Tai
Printed in the U.S.A.   40
First printing January 2011

D0981348

SCHOLASTIC INC.

| New York | Toronto | London | Auckland |
| Sydney | Mexico City | New Delhi | Hong Kong |

It was a beautiful day in Sinnoh. Ash was training one of his Pokémon, Gible.

"All right, Gible. Draco Meteor!" Ash said.

"Gib, gib, gible!" said Gible. A big fireball shot out of its mouth. It zoomed through the air and landed far, far away . . .

. . . right on Piplup's head. *Bop!*

"*Pipluuuuuup,*" Dawn's little blue Pokémon sighed.

"Sorry, Piplup," Ash said. "One more time, Gible!"

Gible fired off two more Draco Meteors. Both landed on Piplup's head — again. *Bonk! Bonk!*

Piplup was starting to get a little mad at Gible.

But when it told Gible how angry it was, Gible just bit Piplup on the head!

"*Piplup, pip!*" Piplup yelled.

But Gible didn't say it was sorry. Now both Piplup's head *and* feelings were hurt.

It was time to get even. Piplup hit Gible with BubbleBeam and Whirlpool.

"Pip, pip, pip, piplup!" it cried.

"Hey, cool it!" Ash said.

Ash, Dawn, and Brock ran over to make sure Gible was okay.

"Don't worry, Gible, you'll get the hang of Draco Meteor," said Ash.

"We know you weren't trying to be mean to Piplup," said Dawn.

"Piplup?" said the little Water-type in disbelief. No one seemed to care about it, not even Dawn.

Piplup felt so lonely, it ran
away into the woods.

It didn't know that Team
Rocket had seen everything from
their hiding place behind a bush.

"Would you get a load of that?"
asked Meowth.

Ash, Dawn, and Brock were
ready to get going. "All right then,
let's move out!" said Brock.
   "Hold on, where's Piplup?"
asked Dawn, looking around.
   Pikachu looked around, too.
"Piplup!" Ash called.

Piplup was still wandering through the woods. It was so upset, it could hardly see. It thought it spotted Dawn in the distance, but it was really an angry Rhyperior!

"Roar!" Rhyperior screamed at Piplup.

Piplup ran away as fast as it could. But it ran right into another kind of trouble — Team Rocket. They were dressed up as the Pokémon Rescue Corps.

"What we do is all for you!"
Jessie told Piplup.

The Pokémon Rescue Corp said
they taught Trainers to be nicer to
their Pokémon.

"Have no fear! Help is here!
We'll dry each tear," they told
Piplup.

Piplup told Meowth none of its friends cared that Gible kept hitting it with Draco Meteor. That's why Piplup had run away.

"Piplupppp!" Dawn's Pokémon wailed, bursting into tears.

The Pokémon Rescue Corps cried
right along with Piplup.
　"We're going to find your friends
and talk some sense into them,"
Jessie promised.

Meanwhile, Ash had sent Staraptor to see if it could find any sign of Piplup.

"Staraptor, did you see Piplup?" he asked.

"Star, star," said Staraptor, shaking its head no.

"Where could Piplup be?" Dawn wondered.

"Gible, will you help us look, too?" asked Ash.

Gible began looking through the woods. It saw something sticking out of a bush and bit it.

"*Roar!*" Rhyperior screamed. That something was its tail!

The big Ground-and-Rock-type started blasting Ash, Dawn, Brock, Pikachu, and Gible.

"AAAAAAAAAAH!" the three Trainers and their Pokémon screamed. They ran away and hid.

Now Rhyperior couldn't find them. But Team Rocket did.

"We're members of the Pokémon Rescue Corps!" said Jessie. "A troubled Pokémon asked us for help. A victim named Piplup!"

The Pokémon Rescue Corps told Dawn and Ash they needed to go through their special training if they wanted Piplup to come back.

"Oh, no!" cried Dawn. She couldn't believe how badly she'd hurt Piplup. Just then, Rhyperior returned. *"Rooooar!"* it shouted, blasting them.

Ash, Dawn, and Brock ran one
way. The Pokémon Rescue Corps
ran the other. Pikachu followed
them. It wanted to find Piplup.
   "Pika, pika!" Pikachu said
when it spotted its friend.

Pikachu tried to get Piplup to follow it back to Dawn, Ash, and Brock.

"Piplup!" Piplup refused. It wanted the Pokémon Rescue Corps to help Pikachu, too.

"Step right this way, Pikachu!"
said Jessie.

Piplup pulled Pikachu into a
little tent. Once inside, the two
Pokémon realized it was a cage.
Piplup and Pikachu were trapped!

"Pikaaaaaaaaaa!" Pikachu tried to zap Team Rocket with Thunderbolt.

"Nice try, but this cage is Pikachu-proof!" Meowth laughed.

"Now where could Piplup and
Pikachu be?" Brock asked.

Gible had an idea. It shot off
Draco Meteor.

"No way," Ash said. The attack
exploded in the distance.

"Yes way!" said Brock. "I'll bet
that Draco Meteor found Piplup!"

This time, Gible's Draco Meteor hit Team Rocket!

"What do you know? It's the Pokémon Rescue Corps!" said Dawn.

"What's going on here?" Ash demanded.

Before Ash, Dawn, and Brock could act, the angry Rhyperior appeared again. It blasted Pikachu and Piplup's cage apart. *"Roar!"*

Dawn ran to Piplup and threw her arms around it. "Piplup, I'm sorry! I was so worried about you!"

"I'm sorry Gible's Draco Meteor kept hitting you," Ash added.

"Gib, gib!" Gible nodded.

"Piplup, pip!" Piplup thanked them for the apology.

Ash turned to Team Rocket.
"I should have known it was you!"
  "Well, prepare to get STOMPED!"
cried Jessie. "Seviper!"
  "*Sssss!*" Seviper hissed.
  "Grotle, I choose you!" Ash
replied. "Energy Ball!"

"Carnivine, you stomp them, too!" James called out.

"Want to get in there, too, Piplup?" asked Dawn.

Piplup stepped right up to battle. Carnivine used Vine Whip. *Pow!*

Piplup tried to fight back with BubbleBeam, but it wasn't enough.

"*Pipluuuup!*" Piplup shouted. Now it was really mad. It used a brand-new move, Hydro Pump.

"Wow!" Dawn cheered.

Swish! Team Rocket blasted off on the waves from Piplup's amazing new move.

Just then, Rhyperior's Trainer appeared. Rhyperior had run away, just like Piplup.

"I'm so sorry, Rhyperior. I was wrong," the Trainer said.

"Roar!" Rhyperior forgave its friend.

Dawn hugged Piplup again. "From now on, let's stay together. What do you say, Piplup?"

"*Pip-lup!*" Piplup agreed with a high five.

Flip over this book to read "Meet Cyndaquil"!